GAME,
SET, AND
MATCH

KINGFISHER
a Houghton Mifflin Company imprint
222 Berkeley Street
Boston, Massachusetts 02116
www.houghtonmifflinbooks.com

First published in 2007
2 4 6 8 10 9 7 5 3 1

LIBRARY OF CONGRESS CATALOGING–IN–PUBLICATION DATA
has been applied for.

ISBN–13: 978-0-7534-6022-1

Printed in India
1TR/0906/THOM/SCHOY/60BNWP/C

GAME, SET, AND MATCH

DONNA KING

KINGFISHER
BOSTON

Chapter 1

"You're a winner, Leo, and you have big dreams."

Carrie Springsteen read her horoscope and sighed.

"You get right where the action is, and don't you just love it when the spotlight is on you!"

No! Carrie thought. *Okay, so I have big dreams of winning in tennis, but that spotlight stuff—no way!*

She sat cross-legged on the grassy slope, reading her magazine. Although she had an August birthday, she didn't see herself as a typical Leo show-off. More of a shy type, really.

"Good shot, Joey!" Hilary called across

the net to the dark-haired kid she was coaching on a nearby court.

Carrie glanced up, sighed again, and then closed her magazine. Joey's session was about to end. *Me next,* she thought.

Her dad came down the steps from the clubhouse. "Hey, Carrie, why aren't you warming up? Come on, pick up your racket—summer vacation may have begun, but we can't have you slouching around."

So she sprang onto her feet, and they headed to the practice court. For ten minutes Carrie hit a ball against the concrete wall.

"Nice work!" her dad told her. "That backhand is really improving. Most grown-ups can't hit the ball that hard. Good job!"

Carrie grinned at him. She felt good— ready to start work with Hilary.

"Hi, Carrie!" The coach greeted her with a wide smile. "How's my star player?"

"Great, thanks." Carrie took up her position across the net from Hilary. She checked her grip and waited for the first ball.

Whack! She hit it in the middle of the strings and returned it fast and low.

"Good shot!" Hilary called.

She nodded and smiled. *Yeah, that felt cool!* Carrie pushed a stray strand of fair hair back from her face and tucked it into her ponytail.

"Again!" Hilary instructed.

Whack! Carrie played the same shot. It zoomed across the net.

"Watch your position. Move your feet!" her dad shouted from the sideline.

Carrie nodded. She crouched and waited. The next ball came toward her, and she hit it hard.

"Nice one!" Hilary said, studying Carrie's backhand.

They'd been playing for almost an hour without a break. Carrie's dad made sure that there was no "slouching around," as he called it.

"Move your feet!" he had yelled over and over. "Come on, Carrie! Run!"

It was hot. She was tired. The palm of her racket hand was sticky with sweat.

"We've got the County Championship coming up this weekend," Martin Springsteen reminded Hilary. "Carrie needs to be at the top of her game."

"She's playing really well," the coach told him. "Her backhand drive is her strongest shot. For a twelve-year-old player, it's the best I've seen."

"Yeah, but she still has to work on the rest of her game." Carrie's dad wanted his golden girl to win. He was determined to make her the best. Ever since Carrie had been able to hold a tennis racket, he'd had his heart set on producing a Grand Slam champion.

Hilary glanced up at the hot sun. "Let's take a break," she suggested.

"No, we haven't had our full hour," Martin argued, checking his watch. "Keep playing, Carrie. You need to practice your serve."

The hour of coaching was over at last. Carrie was in the changing room, getting ready to take a shower. She unlaced her tennis shoes and threw them under the bench. Then she unzipped her dress and loosened her long hair. Turning on the shower, she tilted her head back and let the cool spray sprinkle her cheeks.

Good shot! . . . Nice serve! . . . Game, set, and match to Carrie Springsteen! For her whole life she'd been hearing that stuff.

Carrie's a natural tennis player . . . She has buckets of talent . . . That girl will go far! At five years old Carrie had been spotted by the coach at the fancy club where her mum and dad played tennis. At seven she'd been put into a special program for talented tennis kids.

"Carrie's the one to watch," everyone said. "She's a future Grand Slam champion. She's a star!"

Under the shower Carrie could hear all those voices inside her head.

Okay, at 12 she could hit the ball harder than most adults. She had the longest legs, terrific speed, and lightning-quick reactions. She *was* good!

But lately she didn't go out on the court with a spring in her step like she had last year and all the years before. Carrie took a sharp breath. Maybe she was tennised out!

Take last night, when her best friend, Liv, had called.

"I'm meeting Alice and Mandi in town tomorrow at ten. We're going shopping. Can you come?" she asked.

"Sorry, I can't," Carrie said.

"Okay, don't tell me. You're playing TENNIS." Liv had said the word in capital letters—like, TENNIS MENACE!

"Yeah." Carrie's voice was flat. She was missing out again.

It was the story of her life. Tennis triumph and social life sadness.

Sorry I can't come to the dance/party/ movies . . . I need an early night . . . I'm playing in a tournament. For Carrie, tennis always had to come first.

Sighing, she turned off the shower and got dressed. *Ouch!* She felt a small pain in her thigh, as if she'd pulled a muscle. Pressing her thumbs into the spot, she massaged the ache.

"Hey, Carrie, are you limping?" Hilary asked as she came out of the changing room and onto the balcony overlooking the courts. The coach had been talking with Martin Springsteen while he waited for his daughter to shower and change.

"It's nothing," Carrie answered.

"Are you sure you don't want Hal to take a look?" Hilary asked.

"No, thanks." Hal was the physiotherapist,

but Carrie didn't think the pain was serious.

"Probably just a cramp," her dad guessed, taking her sports bag and heading off down the steps toward the car.

For a few seconds Carrie hung back.

"Is everything okay?" Hilary asked. She knew that Carrie was shy and wouldn't always say what she was thinking.

"Yep." Carrie couldn't think of what else to say. Anyway, her dad was waiting.

"Well, good luck in the under-fourteens this Saturday," Hilary said.

Carrie smiled and nodded.

"The County Championship is a good one to win," her coach reminded her. "It'll get you noticed at a national level— the big time!"

Where the action is—the spotlight! Carrie swallowed hard. "Thanks!"

Hilary gazed at Carrie—at her wide, blue eyes and her sunburned face. "You can do it!" she said quietly.

Carrie gave Hilary a final nod before she

followed her dad down the steps. The ache in her leg was still there, she noticed.

"Your mum called—lunch is ready," her dad said as she got into the car.

She took out her phone and read her text messages as they drove home.

Gd luck on Sat Alice had texted.

Bought cool shirt Liv wrote.

Cool Carrie texted Liv back. Then she stared out the window while her dad talked tactics for the weekend's matches.

"Plenty of topspin on your second serve . . . good, solid baseline play . . . don't take risks . . . wait for your opponent to make the mistakes . . ."

Yeah, Dad, whatever! she thought. She rubbed the ache on the side of her thigh. *But do you know what? Okay, you and Mum want me to be a tennis star more than anything else in the world. But the way I feel right this minute, I wouldn't care if I never picked up another tennis racket in my whole life!*

Chapter 2

"I couldn't decide between them, so I bought both!" Liv said and grinned.

Carrie had stopped by her friend's house to help her choose an outfit for a party. She sat cross-legged on Liv's bed, admiring a glittery shirt.

"Lace or bling?" Liv demanded, twirling in front of her full-length mirror in a white, frilly shirt.

"Bling!" Carrie declared, and Liv tried on the other shirt. "What did Mandi and Alice buy?"

"Alice got a pair of flip-flops, and Mandi bought some bracelets," Liv said, eyeing the other shirt in the mirror. "Silver sequins do it for me!" She flopped down on the bed. "Are you sure you can't make it tomorrow?"

Carrie pulled a glum face. "No way."

"Poor you!" Liv sighed. "Is it the 'T' word again?"

"Yeah, tennis as usual. County Championship."

"Wow! Will you still speak to me after you're rich and famous?"

"It's not that big a deal," Carrie argued. Since her lesson with Hilary two days before, she'd played up her leg injury and skipped two practices. Now her dad was putting pressure on her, pushing her to fit in extra training sessions. "Anyway, I won't win."

"Yeah, you will," Liv told her. "You're tennis-tastic!"

Carrie smiled feebly. "I wish I was coming to the party instead."

"And I wish you were coming too." Liv frowned. "I'm a bit upset about going by myself."

"You won't be by yourself," Carrie

pointed out. "Alice and Mandi will be there."

"Yeah, but . . ."

"Yeah!" They were silent for a second or two, and then Carrie sighed. "I'm freaked out about Saturday," she confessed. "When I think about it, my stomach starts to churn. What if I get knocked out in the first round?"

Liv shook her head. "No way. It won't happen!"

"But what if I have to play Holly Jordan?" Carrie pictured the look of disappointment on her dad's face if she lost to her archrival.

Liv shrugged. "Hey, it's only a game of tennis," she said.

Only a game! Back home, Carrie put on her tennis shoes and picked up her bag of rackets. *Only a nerve-racking, confidence-wrecking game that no one in their right mind would think of taking part in!*

Her mum had managed to squeeze in an

extra coaching session with Hilary, to make up for the ones that she'd missed. Now she was waiting for Carrie at the wheel of the car. "Get a move on, Carrie!" she called.

Carrie dashed downstairs to join her mum.

"You're sure your leg's okay now?" Eva asked as they drove down to the club. Without waiting for an answer, she came in with the advice. "Don't push yourself today, Caz. Save your energy for tomorrow."

Nodding, Carrie waited for her to park the car. She told her stomach to stop tying itself up in knots, then forced herself to go and knock some balls against the wall while her mum went to find Hilary. After five minutes of whacking the ball, she began to feel better.

"Carrie needs to practice her second serve," Eva was telling the coach as the two women joined her. "She gets terrific speed on her first serve, but it's the careful placing of the second that needs work."

"She *does this* . . . she *does that.*" *How come her mum and dad talked about her as if she wasn't there?* Carrie whacked the last ball even harder against the wall.

"We'll work on it," Hilary promised, taking Carrie onto the nearest court.

It was when Carrie was stuck at home later that evening, sitting in her room and watching reality TV, that the tennis blues really hit her.

It was 9 P.M., and everyone was at the party—Liv in her blingy shirt, Mandi and Alice in their flip-flops and bracelets. There would be music and boys. Everyone would be laughing, having a wild time.

Except me! Carrie thought. *I'm sitting here with my stomach doing forward rolls while they're dancing!*

"Time to turn off your light, Carrie!" her dad called up the stairs.

Carrie groaned. Even if she turned off her light, she knew that she wouldn't sleep because she'd be thinking about tomorrow. In her head she would be going through her forehand drive, her overhead smash, and her topspin.

"Light off, Carrie!" her mum warned as she walked by her bedroom ten minutes later. She popped her head around the door. "Everything okay, honey?"

Carrie nodded. She had all of her tennis gear laid out on the floor—her pure-white shoes, her rackets, her cool designer tennis dress—and her alarm was set for 6:30 A.M.

"Sleep well," Eva said, about to close the door.

"Mum!" Carrie's heart was in her mouth as she called her into the room.

"What is it?"

"My leg is hurting again."

"Which one?"

"The same one as before. It still kind of aches." Holding her thigh, Carrie stood up. "When I put weight on it, I get a sharp pain."

Her mother frowned. "Show me exactly where it hurts."

Carrie limped toward her. "Here," she said. She knew that faking a torn muscle would keep her out of the County Championship.

Eva examined the leg and then sat Carrie down on the edge of her bed. Her face was troubled. "I can't see anything wrong," she said quietly. "Are you sure this isn't just something that's going on inside your head?"

Carrie hung her head. She should have known that her mum was too sharp to fall for the fake injury routine.

"Get some sleep," Eva advised, getting up and walking out of the room. "I'm sure you'll be just fine when you wake up tomorrow morning."

Chapter 3

The next morning, Carrie didn't feel fine.

Her stomach was in knots, and her head was a mess. *Jeez, I really don't want to play!* she told her reflection in the bathroom mirror. Then, *What's happening to me? A couple of weeks ago I couldn't wait to get to the County Championship—I was chomping at the bit!*

"Ready, Carrie?" her dad called from downstairs. "I already put your bag and rackets in the car. We need to go!"

"Coming!" she answered, slotting her toothbrush back into the holder. She took a deep breath and squared her shoulders. *Toughen up!* she told herself. *Even if you have to play Holly Jordan in the first round, you're good enough to beat her!*

Okay, so Holly was a top player on the junior circuit. Her backhand was awesome, and she played well at the net. But Carrie had met her in other tournaments and in school events. Although the matches had been tough, Carrie had always come out on top.

She kept telling herself this as her dad drove the 30 miles to the club where the championship was being held.

Then, when they arrived, there were forms to fill in, followed by a loosening-up session on a side court, so it was mid-morning before Carrie got to hear about the draw.

Her mum rushed up to her as she stood on the balcony overlooking the main courts. "You play Kimberley Stevens in the first round, then Mel White or Janey Shawcross in the second. Holly Jordan is in the other half of the draw. You won't play her until the semifinals."

Carrie nodded. She'd just spotted Holly

striding onto the court to play her first opponent. Holly, with her wavy, brown hair and long, slim legs, was looking sure of herself as usual, waiting to see who would serve first, smiling and waving to someone in the small crowd that had gathered.

"You're due on court number three in five minutes," Carrie's mum told her. "Your dad's already down there, waiting for you."

So, Carrie picked up her rackets and went down to the courts, trying to squeeze past the one where Holly was playing without being noticed. Unluckily for her, right at that moment Holly came to the edge of the court to pick up some stray balls. "Hi, Carrie!" she said with a cheesy grin that was meant to stress out her rival. "See you in the semis—if you make it that far!"

Carrie returned the grin. "Yeah, Holly, see you then." Dropping the fake smile, she walked quickly on.

"Hey, Carrie!" On court number three her dad greeted her. He stood behind the umpire's chair, raising his clenched fists like a boxer. "You go, girl!"

At the other side of the net Kimberley Stevens stood ready. She was smaller than Carrie but stocky, with a powerful serve and forehand.

Carrie took up her position, squashing down her stomach flutters and doubts. *I've been here a million times before!* she reminded herself. *I could almost play this game blindfolded!*

Kimberley threw the ball into the air and served. Flashing a forehand return down the line, Carrie won the first point. *Cool!* she told herself. Soon the opening game was over, and Carrie had broken the serve.

"Keep it up, Carrie!" her dad yelled as the players changed ends.

Not too far away, Holly was also serving and smashing her way toward victory. The two gifted girls played on.

"First set to Holly Jordan—six games to two!" Holly's umpire called.

"First set to Carrie Springsteen—six games to one!"

"Holly Jordan leads by four games to love and by one set to love!"

"Game! Carrie Springsteen leads by five games to one and by one set to love!"

"Go, Carrie!" Martin cheered his daughter on toward certain victory.

"Game, set, and match to Holly Jordan—six-two, six-one!"

"Game, set, and match to Carrie Springsteen—six-one, six-love!"

Carrie's dad rushed on court as she shook hands with Kimberley. "Good game!" he told Carrie. "You played well, except your footwork could have been neater and quicker. The next match will be tougher."

Carrie nodded. She wished that just for once her dad could leave out the criticisms and ease off the pressure. She picked up her bag and followed him and her mum off the court.

Holly crossed her path on the way to the

clubhouse. She blocked Carrie's way and locked eyes with her. "Still think you'll make it to the semis?"

Carrie sighed. "I guess," she muttered.

Holly kept on staring. "Yeah, well, you'll have to raise your game if you want to beat me today," she sneered. "I'm so hot, I'm on fire!"

Carrie rocked back on her heels. *Do I?* she asked herself. *Do I really want to beat Holly and get to the final?*

"Okay, honey?" her mum asked, coming back to get her.

Carrie nodded, relieved when Holly spun around and walked off. *Of course I do!* she argued back. *I'm a better player than Holly. I want to win this championship!* She frowned with concentration as she walked on toward the clubhouse.

Her mum was reading the notice board. "Mel White is through to round two, so she's your next opponent."

"Okay, good." Right away her dad

talked tactics. "This kid has a weak forehand. She plays from the baseline. Your job is to get into the net and smash down the forehand side!"

Carrie listened. She'd heard this so many times before—her dad telling her how to win. "Okay, okay," she muttered.

"Hey, are you listening to me? I'm telling you, you need to play aggressively against this girl. No soft shots!"

"Yes, Dad."

He frowned as she turned away. "Stay where you are, Carrie. I haven't finished yet."

You haven't? she thought. Suddenly she got back that feeling that she'd had earlier, of not caring whether or not she ever picked up another tennis racket in her life. *Well, I have finished!* she decided and started to walk away.

Martin reached out to grab her arm and turn her around. "What's wrong with you today?"

The question was like him opening a

door and letting Carrie barge through it. "My leg hurts again," she answered, staring him in the face. *Boy, have I finished!*

"Show me!" he said.

"Here. And here. There's a sharp pain. I told Mum about it."

Her dad's frown deepened. "I didn't notice you limping."

"I'm in agony," she insisted. All around there were the sounds of the tournament— umpires calling scores, crowds cheering and clapping, the zing of tennis balls as they hit tightly strung rackets. But Carrie ignored them all.

"Eva, what's this about Carrie still being injured?" Martin called to his wife.

"I am!" Carrie insisted. She saw Holly hanging around nearby, listening to every word of the conversation, but she was past caring. *Let me out of here!* "Honest, Mum. My leg is killing me!"

Eva put her hands to her face and rubbed her forehead. "She did mention it last night," she told Martin.

He bit his lip and shook his head. "So?" he asked.

"I can't play anymore," Carrie declared, catching the look of glee on Holly's face.

"Chicken!" Holly muttered, loud enough for Carrie to overhear.

Carrie felt her stomach lurch as she turned her back on her gloating rival. This was it—she'd made her decision, and it was time to take a stand. "It's no good, Dad. I'll have to withdraw from the competition!"

Chapter 4

"Carrie dropped out of the County Championship because of this leg injury." Martin Springsteen was talking to Hal, the physiotherapist at the club. It was early on Monday. "Holly Jordan from a club in the south of the county got through to the final and won the under-fourteen event. Carrie slipped down the rankings as a result."

"Yeah, that's a shame." Hal worked on Carrie's leg, bending it and flexing it. "It doesn't seem too bad," he muttered.

"It's worse when I put weight on it," she explained.

"The win yesterday has put Holly ahead of Carrie, even though Carrie's ground strokes and serve are way ahead in terms of technique."

I'm here! Carrie protested silently. *I'm a person, not a machine!*

Hal seemed thoughtful. "I won't do too much more work on it today," he told Carrie, narrowing his eyes and winking at her behind her dad's back. "In fact, I think this muscle strain should fix itself in the next day or two."

"Thanks!" she said hurriedly, almost forgetting to limp as she hopped off the table.

"It was more than a shame," Martin sighed. "Just when Carrie was ready for the breakthrough into the big time!"

"There's always another day." Hal told him, calmly clearing away some towels.

As soon as Carrie and her dad had left, Hal went to look for Hilary. "No way was that a real injury that kept Carrie Springsteen out of the County Championship," he told the coach.

Hilary stared back at him. "You mean she was faking it?"

Hal nodded. "Don't worry. I didn't say anything to Martin, but my theory is that the kid lost her nerve at the last minute and invented the leg injury to keep her out of the competition."

"Oh, boy!" Hilary folded her arms and thought it through. She shook her head. "I've noticed that Carrie has lost a little motivation recently, but I didn't realize she was heading for a crisis." The coach had seen it before—a talented youngster would reach Carrie's age and decide that tennis wasn't where it was at anymore, lured away by clothes, makeup, and other teenage stuff. But Carrie was different; her talent was special.

"Her parents are too pushy," Hal grunted, putting his finger on the core reason.

"Yeah, it would do her some good to get away for a while," Hilary agreed.

"But that isn't going to happen—unless

by any chance you have some kind of magic wand."

"How come?"

"I've just been speaking to Martin. He's set on getting Carrie back up the rankings ASAP."

Hilary took a deep breath and then headed for the exit. "Watch me!" she challenged. "As a matter of fact, I might just have a little bit of magic dust that I can sprinkle over Carrie Springsteen's blonde locks!"

"Will you be home in tonight?" Carrie asked her mum.

"I could be. Is there a reason you want to know?" Eva was making the evening meal—a good balance of protein and carbohydrates, as recommended by the top sports nutritionists.

"Hilary told Dad that she wants to come by." Carrie felt uneasy about the coach's phone call as she and her dad had arrived home. Could it be that Hal had figured out that Carrie had been faking her injury and told Hilary, who now wanted to thrash the whole thing out with her mum and dad?

"Hmm, I wonder what that's about."

"While she's here, we can grab the chance to plan extra coaching sessions," Carrie's dad suggested.

More pressure! Carrie groaned to herself.

She ate her home-cooked spaghetti with meatballs, in spite of her nerves. She didn't have long to wait until the doorbell rang, and Hilary came in, looking relaxed and tanned, bringing the fresh air and the sunshine with her.

"Hi, nice to see you!" Eva began. "This has to be about Carrie's progress, I take it?"

"Or *lack* of it," Martin cut in.

Carrie frowned and tried in vain to fade into the background.

"It sure is," Hilary breezed. "Earlier today I had an interesting idea, made some phone calls, and came up with a new plan of action for Carrie."

Uh-oh, Carrie thought. *She knows I let her down big time, and this is her way of telling me she doesn't want to be my coach anymore!*

"A new plan? What are we doing wrong?" her dad asked edgily.

"Not a thing. Carrie's doing everything right. I wanted to get you all together and put the idea to you so that you could make a quick decision. You have to understand—it would mean a lot of hard work, and Carrie, you would be away from home for four weeks."

"Where would I be?" She looked from her coach to her mum and dad and then back again.

"I got you into a summer school on a scholarship, all expenses paid," Hilary explained.

"What kind of school?" Eva asked.

"A tennis academy."

Martin cleared his throat. "Okay, I get

it. You're saying that Carrie would have four weeks of intensive coaching in a live-in situation?"

Hilary nodded. She looked closely at Carrie's apprehensive face.

"But where exactly would I be?" Carrie asked again. Different thoughts flew through her head: *Am I good enough? Would I be able to hack it? Do I even want to do it?*

The coach gave the broadest of grins. "In the U.S.," she answered. "Florida, at the Ben Sherwood Tennis Academy—one of the best tennis schools in the world!"

Chapter 5

"Oh, wow!" Mandi sighed when she heard the news.

"Lucky, lucky, lucky!" Alice gasped.

The girls were in bikinis, sitting by the side of the water at the town's outdoor pool. They wore their sunglasses and sipped cold, icy cola through straws.

"When do you leave?" Liv asked Carrie.

"Tomorrow," she told them. She'd only had two days to get ready since Hilary had broken the Florida news—frantic days of washing and ironing, shopping, making lists, and packing.

"And how do you feel?" Liv was the only one to notice that Carrie was pretty quiet among all the squeals and shrieks of surprise.

"Nervous!" she confessed. "There'll be kids from all over the world."

"All speaking different languages, and you won't be able to understand any of them," Alice said. "But, hey, the boys will be really cute!"

"Yeah, and Carrie won't even notice!" Mandi said with a laugh. "With her, it'll be all tennis—wham bam, game, set, and match!"

"Back off, Mandi!" Liv muttered. "You only wish it was happening to you."

"Yeah, but Mandi can't even hit the ball over the net!" Alice giggled. "Hey, nice one, Carrie! This could be your big break."

Carrie nodded. "That's what Mum and Dad say."

"You do want to go, don't you?" Liv asked, peering over the top of her sunglasses.

Carrie looked up at the blue sky and then at the big water fountain that was splashing the little kids in the pool. "I suppose I do," she replied quietly.

In spite of her nerves, she felt a tingle of

excitement. Florida, with nonstop sunshine and temperatures of more than 100 degrees. The Sunshine State, with Disney World, speedboats, the Everglades, and bridges across the ocean. Plus, the best tennis players in the world!

"We'll miss you," Carrie's mum said at the airport. She stood with Carrie's dad at the check-in desk, arranging for a member of the cabin crew to keep an eye on her during the flight.

"I'll miss you too," Carrie said in a choked voice. The airport was huge, and she felt very small.

"A trainer from the academy will meet you at the airport when you arrive," her dad reminded her. "Her name is Marie, and she'll be carrying a sign with her details written on it."

What if she's not there? Carrie thought. *I'll be half a world away from home and all alone!* She nodded and swallowed hard.

"Your bag is checked in, but you'll take your rackets on as hand luggage. Don't let them out of your sight," her dad warned.

"Time to go!" her mum said, taking her by the hand. "Remember, at your age both your dad and I would have given up everything for the chance to do what you're doing. So work hard and do your best, okay?"

Carrie nodded again. Her bag had disappeared on a conveyor belt, and she was being told to go to the departure gate. She walked across the vast marble floor toward the security check in a daze.

At the barrier, with tears in her eyes, she hugged her mum and dad and said good-bye.

Nine hours later, on the other side of the Atlantic Ocean, Carrie stepped off the plane with her tennis rackets.

Heat rose from the baked runway. "Sorry," she mumbled as she joined the crush inside the shuttle bus that would take her to the terminal building. "Excuse me. Sorry. Oops!" The rackets got jammed between two large, blonde ladies.

"Hey, honey. No problem!" one replied, smiling at the shy English girl.

Must look out for Marie! Carrie told herself. *Must not be scared of giant buildings and security men with guns. Must keep my cool.*

Leaving the bus to join a long line for immigration control, at last she came out into the vast concourse where hundreds of people held up signs to greet travelers from the U.K.: "Mr. Brown, Metropole Hotel"; "Dr. Sanders, Medicare"; "Randy Allbright, Disney".

Dazed and confused, Carrie scanned the signs, convinced that Marie from the Ben Sherwood Tennis Academy wasn't among them.

"Hi!" a bright voice said. A small, dark-haired woman approached with a broad smile. "You must be Carrie!"

"How did you know?" Carrie began

and then blushed. *Hey, the rackets make it obvious, stupid!*

Soon Marie had whisked her off into an air-conditioned silver SUV, and they hit the highway.

"We'll be in time for dinner," Carrie's driver told her chattily. "Then you'll want to go to your room and get your head down for a good night's sleep. The program begins tomorrow with a half-hour of dynamic stretching, followed by two-and-a-half hours of intensive work on technical skills and footwork. After lunch we address offense and defense, plus specialty shots and tactics. Evenings, you get time for free play and matches."

"Wow," Carrie muttered. No time for slouching around—her dad would have been delighted.

"We have fifteen top-notch kids at the summer school for this course," Marie told her, easing through a built-up area and onto the open road. "Ten Americans and five

Europeans. Ben has high hopes for you, Carrie, because you're coming to us on a scholarship. Your coach at home has e-mailed amazing recommendations."

Thanks, Hilary! Carrie groaned inwardly. *As usual, no pressure there!*

"The others are paying one thousand dollars a week to be here," Marie added in a confidential tone. "Not including the Pro Max add-ons, like videotaping your matches, massages, and private lessons with Ben Sherwood himself!"

"This can't be happening!" Carrie said out loud.

Her room at the academy overlooked two massive outdoor pools. The pool area was lined with palm trees, and beyond it there were tennis courts as far as the eye could see. Or not quite—because if Carrie went out onto her balcony and looked beyond the pools and tennis complex, she caught glimpses of a white beach and a dazzling blue sea.

She sighed and sat down on her bed. The room had a TV, a fridge, a shower, and a walk-in closet, but she didn't feel really excited because there was no one to say, "Hey, look at this plasma screen!" or "This sun lounger is so cool!" to.

There was only Marie, showing her the gym and the saunas, and a loud Texan kid named Leon—"Hey, how come you're so pale? Oh yeah, you're English!"—plus a tanned French girl named Danielle, whom she'd met at dinner.

"I miss Paris *et mes amis!*" Danielle had complained loudly. "In Paris I do shopping. Here there is only Mickey Mouse!"

"Don't listen to her," Leon had advised Carrie. "She's always shooting her mouth off. Hey, and what did French dudes ever invent, except cheese?"

After dinner Leon had shown Carrie the way back to her room and said that he would come get her at 6:30 A.M. "Be ready," he'd warned. "With Ben, being late isn't an option!"

Now, Carrie kicked off her shoes and shook her head. "No, this isn't happening!" she said again—the airports, the big interstate highway, the plush academy, and the great Ben Sherwood. She lay back, and almost before her head touched the pillow, she was asleep.

"Don't kid yourselves," the world-famous coach announced when he met his students the following morning. "This is the toughest youth academy in professional sports!"

Carrie quaked in her brand-new tennis shoes. Ben Sherwood was lean, fit, and perma-tanned, with shaved gray hair and trendy sunglasses. He scared the pants off her.

"This is a prison!" Danielle declared under her breath.

"It's awesome!" Leon argued.

Both had already spent four weeks at the school the previous summer and acted as if they were part of the furniture.

"There are three words you have to remember if you want to succeed 'The Sherwood Way,'" Ben went on. "Work, work, and work!"

A girl next to Carrie grimaced and shuffled uneasily.

I could be at home lounging by the pool with Liv, Mandi, and Alice. Carrie thought. *We could be discussing shades of lipstick!*

"By the end of this summer school, you will all be incredibly fit, focused, and disciplined athletes," their coach continued.

By his side, Marie looked up at her boss, smiled, and nodded.

"We get you up at six-thirty A.M., we make you stretch, run, and do push-ups. Then we make you hit lots of balls."

What am I doing here? Carrie asked herself. *There I was, rapidly going off the whole tennis idea. And here I am now, halfway across the world, in this nightmare sports school!*

Ben Sherwood strode up and down the

row of young students. He spotted Carrie and stopped. "Welcome to America," he told her. "You traveled a long way to be here. Did you meet your fellow countryman yet?"

Slowly working out what the great man meant, she shook her head.

Marie stepped forward. "Hey, let me make the introductions!"

Carrie looked down the line to see a girl break away and walk toward her. Straightaway, with a jolt of surprise, she recognized the tall figure and wavy, brown hair of Holly Jordan.

Smiley Marie did the honors. "Carrie, do you know Holly from back home? Holly—Carrie. Carrie—Holly!"

"I guess you two don't like each other, huh?" Leon got Carrie off to one side after Ben Sherwood's opening speech.

"I didn't even see her there!" Carrie said and blushed. "I was so uptight about meeting Ben for the first time. Anyway, what makes you think I don't like Holly?"

Leon grinned, rolling a piece of gum around in his mouth. "Come on, it's not rocket science—the way you looked at her and she looked at you!"

"Holly's okay," Carrie protested. Of course, she hadn't seen her since her own meltdown at the County Championship, which Holly had won in grand style. She recalled the look of glee on Holly's face as Carrie had made her decision to withdraw and realized that the last thing she wanted to do right now was spend four weeks at summer school with her rival.

"Who's the better player?" Leon wanted to know.

Carrie shrugged. "Holly just won a big tournament. I had to pull out because of an injury." Out of the corner of her eye she saw Holly whispering with the French girl, Danielle.

"That means you're better!" Leon

declared with a laugh, before Marie pulled him into line and took everyone off to the gym.

"Step in to take the serve early!" Ben Sherwood coached Carrie during her first private session later that day. Her practice partner was Leon.

She felt sweat trickle down her neck as the Florida sun beat down.

"You have super-fast reactions," the coach pointed out. "You can move in and take your opponent by surprise."

Carrie did as she was told, taking the next serve from Leon much sooner than before. Her return flew low and fast over the net, leaving him stranded on the baseline.

"Good job!" Ben praised her and then gave her another tip. "Rule number one when you're on court—never take a backward step! Always move in, put pressure on your opponent—attack!"

Carrie nodded. This time she not only

took Leon's serve mega early, but she followed up her return with a rush to the net. Her next shot blasted Leon off the court.

"Yeah, she learns fast!" Ben told Marie. "Keep her on the Pro Max program."

"For free?" his assistant asked.

Ben nodded. "She has the talent to turn professional when she's older," he said. "But with this kid, it's gonna come down to whether or not she has the mental toughness. I can tell you that right now!"

Chapter 6

"Believe me, Ben has his finger on the pulse of the whole tennis world," Leon told Carrie.

They were taking a lunch break the following day, walking along the soft, white sand. A sea breeze was cooling Carrie down after her one-on-one session with the top coach. "He scares me," she admitted to Leon.

"Yeah, he scares everyone—even the top pros."

The sand was warm on the bare soles of Carrie's feet. She wandered toward the water and began to paddle. "He acts like we're in the army."

"Yeah, you don't say 'no' to Ben

Sherwood." Lazily wading into the water after Carrie, Leon stuffed his hands into the pockets of his loose, patterned shorts.

"Just like my dad," Carrie muttered and then wished she'd kept that thought to herself.

Leon glanced her way. For once he didn't follow up with a question. "This is my second summer school," he told her. "While other kids fool around in camp, my parents pay for me to come here, and I get to do it 'The Sherwood Way!'"

"Lucky you!" Carrie smiled sarcastically. It seemed like Leon had the same kind of parents as she did. She liked his laid-back style, even though the patterned shorts suggested that he could definitely use a style makeover.

"Yeah, lucky me. It's my job to live their dream!" His laugh sounded hollow. "And y'know, Ben has you marked down as a top player of the future," he reminded Carrie. "Like I say, he has his finger on the pulse. He knows raw talent when he sees it!"

"It's so weird, watching yourself play on camera!" Carrie said to Danielle.

The two girls had played a practice match that Maria had videotaped. Carrie had come out on top by six games to three.

Danielle shrugged and sulked.

"No one beat her before you came along," Leon explained, without bothering to lower his voice.

Danielle narrowed her eyes and made a *puh!* sound.

Oops! Carrie saw that she'd made an enemy of the French girl without even trying. She fixed her attention back on the TV screen and studied her service action—throw the ball high and straight, shift the weight onto the back foot, swing the racket in a deep downward curve, bring it up from behind, and smack the ball hard.

"Good serve!" Marie commented.

At the back of the room Danielle went into a huddle with Holly Jordan. She whispered something that made Holly laugh.

"You picked out Danielle's weak spot and put pressure on it." Marie went on praising Carrie's tactics until the video ended and the group split up.

"Yeah, you think she'd do something with her hair!" Holly said to Danielle as they left the room and headed for the pool. She smirked in Carrie's direction.

Carrie swallowed hard, pretending not to notice. *What's wrong with my hair?* she cried inwardly.

"And did you see her shoes?" Danielle scoffed.

What's wrong with my shoes? Carrie panicked. Before she could figure it out, Leon and a couple of other kids corralled her and dragged her to the pool.

"Relax!" Leon told her. "Time to hang

out!" He ran toward the water and dived in, followed by a tiny eight-year-old boy named Bobby and a dark-haired girl named Maya. The triple splash reached Carrie, who slipped out of her tracksuit and followed them into the pool.

She dived long and shallow and surfaced next to Bobby.

"Cool dive!" Bobby told her, launching himself into a messy back crawl.

"Hey, stop that!" Danielle yelled from her lounger. "Some people don't like to get wet!"

Leon winked at Carrie and then smoothly disappeared below the surface. He came up close to where Danielle and Holly sat, surfacing like a dolphin and hauling himself out of the pool.

"Leon, stay away!" Danielle warned. She jumped up and ran to a safe distance.

By this time, Bobby and Maya had joined in the fun. They climbed out of the pool with water streaming off of them, helping Leon surround Holly.

Holly looked up from her lounger and gasped. "No way!" she protested when she realized their plan.

"Time to test the water!" Leon said and grinned, grabbing Holly's arm.

She resisted, but Bobby, Maya, and Leon laughed and dragged her to the edge of the pool.

"Yee-haw!" Leon yelled as they gave a final push.

Splash! Holly hit the water and disappeared. She came up next to Carrie, gasping like a fish.

Carrie stared at Holly's streaming hair and open mouth.

"You!" Holly gasped.

Carrie shook her head. "Don't look at me!"

Bobby, Maya, and Leon stood by the side of the pool and laughed.

"You *made* them do it!" Holly spluttered angrily. "Just because I won the championship—this is your idea of a joke!"

"No!"

"Yeah, it's your way of getting back at me!" Holly insisted, turning her back and swimming away.

"Why would I want to do that?" Carrie asked, trying to follow but stopping when Holly kicked a storm of foaming white water in her face.

"Because I'm the County Champion, and you're not!" Holly declared. She reached the metal steps and pulled herself clear of the water. "Don't pretend you weren't scared stiff of playing me in the semis, Carrie Springsteen!" she spat out. "That's why you faked an injury. You're a no-talent loser, and the sooner you face it, the better!"

"What did I do?" Carrie asked Leon after Holly and Danielle had stalked off to their rooms.

"Zilch. Big fat zero," he assured her. "Forget it."

Easier said than done, she thought, watching Leon and Bobby jump back into the pool with maximum splash. How come it was so easy to make enemies here at the academy? First Danielle, and now Holly. She sighed and shook her head.

Later, in her room, she called home. Her mum answered the phone.

"How are you doing? Did you meet the great Ben Sherwood yet? What's he like? How's the coaching program? How many kids are in the course?"

The questions came in like an avalanche. Carrie answered them with, "Good. Yep. Cool. Good. Fifteen."

Then her dad came on. "Carrie, did you play a match yet? Did you win? Did they put you on the Pro Max program?"

"Yep. Yep. Yep."

"Great!" her dad said. "You're going to be a Grand Slam champ before you know it!"

Carrie gritted her teeth. "Don't hold

your breath," she warned.

"What do you mean?"

"I mean, everyone here is pretty good," she explained. "Holly Jordan is here, and a couple of French girls, plus a Russian boy and . . ."

"Holly's there?" her dad echoed. "Did she get a scholarship?"

"I don't know. Probably not."

"But you did!" he reminded her. "You've got more talent in your little finger than Holly Jordan has in her whole body!"

"Dad!" Carrie protested. *Lay off me, please. Give me a break!*

"Remember, you gotta kick butt, as the Americans say!" he laughed, handing the phone back to her mum.

Sighing, Carrie told her that the food was okay and that her room overlooked the pools. The usual stuff. What she didn't tell her was that she was stressed and homesick. Oh, and two of the kids in the course already hated her.

"What's the weather like?" her mum asked.

"Scorching."

And that was it—the end of things to talk about. Carrie promised to call again soon and hung up.

I hate it here! she thought, going onto the white veranda and gazing out onto a red-gold sunset. Other people would call it paradise, but she wanted out. *I can't hack it. I want to go home!*

Home was a million miles away, Carrie realized early the next morning when she went to her locker to get her things.

The locker door was open, which was weird because she was sure that she'd closed it the night before.

"What's wrong?" Maya asked, sleepily tying her sneakers before she headed to the gym.

Carrie looked inside her locker and saw that it was empty. "Who took my stuff?" she asked slowly, still a bit dazed by the early start.

"Don't look at me!" Holly protested loudly from the far corner of the room.

Next to her, Danielle gave one of her smirks. Then she looked thoughtful. "Holly, didn't you say you saw one of the boys in the girls' locker room late last night?"

Her friend nodded. "I caught Leon sneaking out. I didn't say anything, though."

Carrie frowned. Surely Leon wouldn't set her up in this way. She knew that he was into practical jokes, but why would he raid her locker?

Anyway, the important thing was to find her shorts, T-shirt, and sneakers. She began searching on the floor and behind the lockers while the room emptied and she was left alone.

Her things were nowhere to be found.

Realizing that she was late for the early-morning workout, she decided to run back to her room for her spare shorts and shoes. On the way she bumped into the one person she didn't want to see.

Ben Sherwood was coming back from his jog along the deserted beach. He stopped, tapped his watch, and frowned at Carrie. "Six forty-five!"

Breathlessly, she began to explain, but he shook his head. "Don't give me any excuses," he warned her. "Remember the work ethic behind 'The Sherwood Way' and don't be late again."

Groaning, she hurried on. "If it really was Leon who stole my stuff, I'll kill him!" she muttered to herself. Quickly getting changed, she dashed to the gym and looked for Leon.

"That wasn't funny!" she accused the joker.

Leon was doing push-ups. "Thirty-three, thirty-four . . ."

"I said, that wasn't funny!" Carrie repeated. She began her push-ups in the space next to him. "One, two, three . . .

Stealing someone's stuff isn't my idea of a joke!"

"Thirty-seven, thirty-eight. I don't get it. Who's stealing what around here?"

"You! The stuff in my locker! Holly saw you last night. Eight, nine, ten . . ."

Leon breathed hard. "Forty, forty-one. Ha-ha, very funny!" he muttered.

Suddenly, Carrie lost count and gave up. She caught a sideways glimpse of Holly and Danielle calmly lifting weights.

"Huh!" she gasped, collapsing on the floor. "Those two set me up!"

"Forty-five, forty-six . . ." Leon went on. "Take it easy!" he declared. "It's true—I didn't steal your stuff, and Danielle and Holly most likely did. But don't get dragged down to their level. You're better than them, and you should remember it!"

"That's easy for you to say," Carrie muttered. Her face was hot and flushed as she began her push-ups again. *How sneaky!* she thought, picturing the two girls snickering and giggling as they played their trick. *How low-down and sneaky was that!*

Chapter 7

"It's a confidence thing." Marie tried to get the message across to Carrie in her next coaching session. Carrie was three days into the course and struggling.

"Wanting to win is vital. Some people call it the killer instinct."

Carrie nodded. She stood close to the net, receiving high balls from the coach, which she smashed back.

"Good technique!" Marie told her. "Great shot! Fabulous angle! Good job!"

Carrie came off court feeling better and went for a cool shower. When she came out of the locker room, she found Holly hanging around on the porch.

Uh-oh! Carrie bristled. She looked

around for Danielle, didn't see her, and was shocked when Holly smiled and said hi.

Carrie nodded back.

"I'd like to talk," Holly confessed awkwardly.

"Go ahead, talk." Alarm bells were ringing inside Carrie's head. "What about?"

Slowly, Holly took a pair of shoes out of her bag.

"My sneakers!" Carrie gasped. Then she recognized the T-shirt and denim shorts that Holly pulled out next. "I knew it was you and Danielle who stole my stuff!"

Holly blushed and then nodded. "Not really me. It was Danielle's idea. I joined in for a laugh."

"Well, it was *so* not funny!" Carrie retorted, snatching back her things.

Holly sighed. "Yeah, I'm sorry, Carrie. I was a bit of witch. But Leon was partly to blame, too."

"Why do you say that?" From the shade of the porch Carrie and Holly watched a dozen kids hitting balls out on the courts while Marie and Ben yelled instructions.

"He has this thing about Danielle," Holly explained. "He's always pestering her and trying to look big in front of her. She's told him to stop, but it doesn't make any difference. Now she's fed up with it."

Carrie thought about this for a while. "So she tried to set him up over my stuff?"

"To teach him a lesson. I went along with it, but I said from the start that she should've left you out of it."

"Totally!" Carrie agreed. Okay, so Leon strutted his stuff in front of Danielle, and Danielle didn't like it. It would be just like her to try to get him into trouble. Carrie thought it through and decided to accept Holly's apology. After all, despite the bad feeling at the County Championship, they were the only two Brits in the course. Now they could chat about home and share stuff. "I don't like having enemies, so I'm glad we're friends," she told her.

"Me, too." Holly's grin was stiff. "I have to go and play now. But I wanted to make sure that there are no hard feelings."

Carrie nodded. "Good, I'm glad. See you later."

"Yeah, see you later . . ." Holly echoed, walking out into the sunshine, her face changing in an instant. ". . . sucker!" she muttered as she strode away.

"Holly Jordan is into mind games!" Leon decided. "She and Danielle are the same."

"So you don't have a . . . kind of . . . a secret thing about Danielle?" Carrie asked.

She'd gone to find Leon after his evening match against Michael Lewis, a top junior from New York. It had been played in fierce heat, and Leon had won seven-five, six-four. Now he and Carrie were chilling out again on the beach.

Leon laughed out loud. "Do I have a secret thing about Danielle?" he echoed.

"So, you don't?" Carrie asked. *Wow, this is complicated!*

He laughed so much that he had to hold his stomach. "*In Paris I do shopping!*" He mimicked the French girl's voice and accent. "She figures Texas is still stuck in the days of the Wild West and ten-gallon hats!"

"Isn't it?" Carrie said and grinned.

"Yeah, and England is a small island hanging off the edge of Europe!"

"So?" Carrie took a deep breath of sea air. "What do you mean by mind games?"

Leon looked at her as if she'd been born yesterday. "Call me mean and cynical," he said, "but I'd say this is all about Holly messing up your mind by faking friendship."

"Why?"

"So you trust her and your guard is down. Then she'll drop you like a brick."

"But why?" Carrie still didn't get it.

"To make you feel bad. So you reach the point where you want to bury your head in the sand!"

"Then my concentration goes," Carrie realized. "And I can't play my best tennis."

Leon grinned and nodded. "Now you got it!"

Nasty! Carrie thought. There was still a piece of her that wanted to stay friends with Holly. "But how can you be sure?"

There was a long pause while Leon stared out across the blue ocean. "Because that's exactly what Danielle did to me last summer," he answered. "Then I played her in the academy tournament final, and she kicked my butt!"

On Monday evening of the first week Carrie was due to play Maya. It was the first match of the knockout competition that would eventually decide who was the top player in the course.

"Good luck, Caz!" Carrie's mum told her over the phone.

"Go out there and win!" her dad ordered. "Remember, Carrie Springsteen is the one to watch!"

Carrie thought through the points she'd already learned from 'The Sherwood Way.' Work, work, work. Always move forward; never move back. Develop the killer instinct. Oh, and, as she'd learned from Leon, trust no one!

"Good luck, Carrie!" Holly called from her balcony as Carrie headed for the locker room. Danielle stood and watched from the room next door to Holly's.

Carrie waved uneasily. Was Holly fake, or was she genuine? She had no time to consider it as she hurried to get ready.

"See you on court in five minutes," Marie told her on the locker-room porch.

Take the serve early! Carrie reminded herself. She opened her locker to take out her rackets—only to find that it was empty! "Not again!" she groaned. Once was bad enough, but this trick played on her twice made her want to sit down and cry.

Carrie flew back to Holly's room.

"Okay, give me my rackets!" she demanded. "This is *so* not funny. Where are they? Give them to me!"

Holly stood in a turquoise sarong and bikini top. "What are you talking about?" she asked.

Next door, Danielle wore her shocking pink bikini and special smirk.

"Someone's taken my rackets from my locker!" Carrie cried. "How am I supposed to play my match?"

"Use mine," Holly offered quickly—*too* quickly, Carrie thought later. But what could she do? No way could she be late for her match.

So she grabbed the racket that Holly handed her over the rail of the balcony and raced back to the tennis courts. She ran straight to her service end while Marie climbed into the umpire's chair and Maya took up her position on the other side.

"Two minutes to knock up, and then we start the match," Marie told them.

Carrie watched Maya drive a forehand toward her. She swung Holly's racket to return it. *Plunk!* The ball fell dead at her feet.

She frowned and studied the racket head. *Two broken strings—thanks a lot, Holly!*

"Try to be better prepared in the future," Marie told her with a frown.

Carrie didn't argue back. What was she going to do now?

"Here, try these," a voice said.

She looked up to see Leon jogging across the court toward her and handing her two of his own top-quality rackets.

"I told you—it's about mind games," he reminded her. "Don't let Holly Jordan get away with it!"

Taking a deep breath, Carrie nodded.

"Play!" Marie instructed.

"Go, Carrie!" Leon's voice carried across the court.

It was one set–all and five games–all. Maya was on her best form. Carrie was trying everything to beat her, but so far the match was even.

"Go, Maya!" Danielle had come to watch. She stood and cheered on Carrie's rival.

Soon a group of half-a-dozen kids were rowdily clapping at every shot.

Carrie gritted her teeth as she prepared to serve. Sweat trickled down her face and neck. She could hardly grip the racket because of the heat.

Across the net Maya crouched, ready to receive.

"Maya, Maya, Maya!" Danielle led a chant that Bobby and a few others joined in.

Mind games! Carrie threw the ball into the air, served, and watched it crash into the net. She tried a second time, and the ball went in. Maya returned it hard down Carrie's backhand side. Carrie hit it across court, fast and low. Maya stretched but couldn't reach it.

"Fifteen-love," Marie called.

More spectators gathered—some grown-ups from the adult course, plus Ben Sherwood himself.

Carrie noticed him and felt her nerves jangle. As she prepared to serve the next point, she overheard Danielle claiming that Carrie's foot had crossed the baseline when she'd served her second serve.

"It was a foot fault!" Danielle insisted. "No way should Carrie be ahead!"

The snide challenge wrecked Carrie's concentration. She threw the ball crooked and hit it awkwardly, giving Maya the chance to move in and pass her crosscourt.

"Nice shot!" Danielle sang out.

"Fifteen-all!" Marie leaned down from her chair for a word with Ben.

Carrie wiped the sweat from her forehead. Her head was all messed up—first from the missing rackets and broken strings and now from Danielle's catty comments. She felt the match slipping away from her.

Two feeble points later, she was 15-40 down.

Ben passed a comment to Marie and shook his head. Danielle led the cheers for Maya.

If I lose this point, I might as well say good-bye to the match! Carrie told herself. *I'll soon be out of the tournament!*

"You can do it, Carrie!" Leon yelled from beyond the wire fence.

His voice gave her a boost. She served two aces to draw level.

"Foot fault!" Danielle cried.

Marie ignored the protest.

Two more points to win my serve! Carrie threw the ball perfectly and served deep. Maya snatched her return, allowing Carrie to move in on it and volley it out of reach.

One more point!

"Go, Maya!" Danielle chanted.

Carrie concentrated hard. She served again—so fast that Maya didn't even get her racket to it.

"Game!" Marie called. "Carrie leads by six games to five, one set–all."

Nerves got to Maya during her final service game. She served a double fault, then at 30–40 down she served another and crashed out at seven-five.

Carrie and Maya shook hands over the net. Ben Sherwood nodded without showing any expression and then walked on to watch another match. Carrie grinned at Leon as she gave him his rackets back.

"Nice work." He took Carrie off to one side. "Did you tell Holly where she could stick her broken racket?" he muttered in his Texan drawl.

She laughed and shook her head. "Not yet. That was another mega mean trick, though."

"But this time you came through."

"Yeah, I came through!" she sighed, heading to the locker room, where—surprise, surprise!—she found her tennis rackets innocently propped up against a bench.

I came through! she thought again as she turned on the shower and enjoyed the cool spray.

And then, letting her head clear under the cool, pure water, she had a major breakthrough—*it's not so much the person on the other side of the net I have to beat,* she realized. *Like Leon said, it's the others who mess with your mind. The Hollys and the Danielles of the tennis world—the underhand ones who will stoop to anything to make sure that they win!*

"Wow, that feels good!" she murmured, not talking about the shower, but about her suddenly clear head. She dried herself off and made a quick exit from the locker room, speeding to her bedroom to call her mum and dad.

"Hi, honey!" Her mum answered the phone as usual. "How are you?"

"Good," Carrie said. She wanted to tell her about the big breakthrough. "Actually, better than good."

Quickly her dad came on the phone.

"Did you win a match?" he asked eagerly.

"Yeah, I did. But . . ."

"That's my girl!" Martin crowed. "Who did you beat? Was it Holly Jordan?"

"No, Dad. Anyway, that's not why I'm feeling happy."

"Who was it then?" he interrupted. He wanted all the details—scores, tactics, who she played next, and so on. "Was Ben Sherwood watching?" he asked finally.

Every time her dad asked a question, Carrie felt like a boxer taking a punch. *Oof—oof!* "Dad, would you put Mum back on?" she pleaded.

Then her mum rushed in with, "Well done, honey! Your dad and I are so proud of you!"

Carrie took a deep breath. She had to say this next thing straight out, no messing around. "Listen, Mum, I'm not actually doing this for you!"

There was a gasp followed by a pause, and then, "What do you mean?"

"I'm finished with that, Mum. If I carry on playing tennis, you and Dad have to know that I'm not doing it to please you. Mainly, I'm doing it for myself!"

How good did that feel? Carrie was soaring now, way above all those doubts and worries, free—telling it like it was.

"Of course," her mum said hesitantly.

"It's *my* life."

"Yes, Carrie, we know that."

"Do you, Mum? Do you really? And does Dad?"

"Let me talk to her." Martin grabbed the phone. He sounded tense. "We only want the best for you—that's all we've ever wanted. So don't start throwing it back in our faces."

Ouch! There was the old heavyweight punch again! Carrie almost caved in, but she came back at her dad, far away in old England. "It's not what *you* want anymore, Dad. It's what *I* want!"

"Don't be cheeky, Carrie."

"I'm not—honestly! But Dad, you have to stop push-push-pushing me all the time. Like, for instance, at the County Championship—I felt awful after you pushed me so hard."

"Only to get the best performance out of you," he insisted.

He still didn't get it. "No, it doesn't work like that. You have to back off," Carrie said firmly.

"Or else what?"

She took another deep breath. "Or else I quit tennis!" she announced, hardly able to believe what she'd just said. "If you don't agree to let me do it my way, I pack my bags, and I'm on the first plane out of here!"

Chapter 8

After her victory on the Monday evening and the standoff with her parents, Carrie settled into a routine of early stretching and workouts, followed by a morning of hitting balls in the fierce Florida sun under the eagle eyes of Marie and Ben.

She felt good, but she still took the chance to let off steam. "This is harder than the hardest of all hard-core boot camps!" she wrote on her postcard to Alice. "What did I do to deserve this?!!!"

In the afternoons she was videotaped, and then Marie would play the tape and point out all her faults.

"Your footwork needs more work, she would say. Or, "You're way out of position to receive this shot."

"It's torture!" Carrie wrote to Mandi on the back of a card showing palm trees and white sand. "I know you won't believe me, because it looks mega perfect. But I've never worked so hard in my life!"

Evenings would involve either match play or fooling around by the pool in rare moments of leisure.

"Have lost three pounds and am getting skinny," she wrote to Liv on a card with a bottlenose dolphin leaping out of the clear, blue sea. "Thinking of you partying without me! Luv, Caz xxx."

By Friday she felt like she'd lived all of her life at the academy and that England, her family, and friends were all a dream.

"There are losers and winners in this life," Ben Sherwood told his students at the end of their first week. They sat together in the clubhouse, muscles aching, skin tingling from the sun. "It's my job to turn you all into winners, no matter what it takes!"

"Does that include stealing a player's rackets before the start of a match?" Carrie whispered to Leon and little Bobby. She was determined to make a joke of Holly and Danielle's nasty trick, instead of letting it get to her.

"Hey, wow! Who stole your rackets?" Bobby wanted to know.

Ben stopped his lecture, and everyone turned to stare. Danielle glared at Carrie defiantly.

"I don't know for sure," she muttered to the excitable little kid. "All I know is that my rackets disappeared from my locker."

"Whoa!" Ben raised his hand to demand attention. "Carrie, did you tell anyone about this?"

Quickly, she shook her head. Without proof, she knew that she had to keep her suspicions to herself.

Holly leaned over and anxiously whispered to Danielle.

Ben shook his head. "If anything like this happens again, I want you to report it," he told Carrie. "We can't have you circulating these rumors unless you can back it up with evidence."

She squirmed. Somehow the coach had done a good job of turning her into the guilty one.

Nearby Holly and Danielle settled back into their seats, arms folded, making a big show of lazily chewing gum.

"The same goes for everyone," Ben declared. "If something bad happens, don't sit on it. Come to me or Marie and let us help you sort it out."

He went on with the team talk, leaving Carrie hot and bothered, until Danielle stopped chewing and raised her hand.

"Yes, Danielle. Do you have a question?" Ben asked.

"Not a question exactly," she began. "It's about something you said earlier."

All eyes turned to the French girl, whose

voice was lower than usual. They waited in suspense for her to continue.

"Okay," Ben said slowly. "What did I say?"

"That we must come to you with a problem."

He nodded. "Go ahead."

"It happened this morning—I can't find my necklace."

A stir went around the group. Some of the kids were impatient, others curious. Carrie felt a flutter of anxiety as the French girl went on. "The necklace is made from gold, with a diamond. I take it off to go in the shower. When I go to put it on again, it is not there."

Maya nudged Carrie, eyes wide, mouth open. Bobby grew excited again. "Oh, wow!" he said. "How much did it cost? Was it more than one thousand dollars?"

"How come she wears a stupid diamond necklace to play tennis?" Leon cut in, loud enough for Carrie, Holly, and Danielle to hear, though Ben hadn't caught what he'd said.

The coach frowned. "Come and talk to me when we're done here," he instructed Danielle.

He rounded off his talk with more reminders about mental toughness. Meanwhile, Carrie's feeling of unease grew.

"What's wrong with you?" Leon asked her after the talk was over and Danielle had gone off with the coach. "Why the long face?"

"Call me suspicious," she began, "but I have a feeling that Danielle is about to set me up again—this time over this necklace thing."

"How come?"

"Besides Holly, I know I was the only one in the locker room when she took her shower."

Leon nodded. "Gotcha. Ben's gonna ask who else was there, and she's gonna point the finger."

"I didn't go anywhere near the necklace!" Carrie protested.

"Yeah, I believe you. It looks like another one of her mind games," Leon muttered. "But how come she's so down on you right this minute? Why not yesterday or next week some time?"

"Because . . ." Carrie seized his arm and dragged him off to inspect the notice board that showed the next round of the knockout competition, ". . . who am I playing tomorrow evening?"

Leon ran his forefinger down the list until he came to Carrie's name and the name of her opponent. "Danielle!" he gasped. "Now I get it."

Another setup. A new reason for her confidence and concentration to zoom down to rock bottom.

"I didn't think even Danielle would stoop so low," Carrie groaned. "But it turns out I was wrong!"

Chapter 9

On Saturday morning Carrie got the message that she'd been dreading.

"Ben would like to see you in his office," Marie told her after the morning workout. Her expression gave nothing away.

Carrie was trembling as she climbed the steps to the clubhouse, walked along the balcony, knocked on the head coach's door, and went in.

"Yeah, hi, Carrie," Ben said, busy with his computer. He tapped some keys and then logged off. "Sit down. We need to talk."

She sat and waited.

"You know that theft of property is serious," he began, clasping his fingers together and resting his hands on his desk.

"So I want you to think hard and tell me the truth about what happened in the girls' locker room yesterday morning."

"Nothing happened!" she cried, her stomach churning. "I didn't see anything, and no way did I take Danielle's necklace!"

"Who said you did?" Ben countered. "But listen—Danielle has given me the exact circumstances. She says for sure that only you and Holly Jordan were there when she took her shower, when the piece of jewelry went missing."

"That's true," Carrie admitted. *This is so not fair!* she cried inwardly. *Why take her word for it? Can't you see that she's probably making the whole thing up?*

"So I already talked to Holly," Ben explained, more severe than any school principal. "She gave me her word that she didn't touch the necklace."

"Me neither!" Carrie insisted.

Ben stared at her, forcing eye contact. "I'd like to believe you," he said quietly.

"However, Danielle filled me in on some more background. Didn't you accuse her and Holly outright of stealing your rackets, which coincidentally showed up later the same day?"

"No, I never did! Well, not exactly . . . I kind of thought . . . I went to Holly's room and asked her where my rackets were." Carrie trailed off and let her gaze drop to the carpet.

Ben tapped the table. "Why did you do that?" he asked.

"Because Danielle had already stolen my things and made me late for my workout. Holly confessed it." Carrie thought that if she told the truth, it would convince the coach.

"Jeez!" Ben tutted. "You girls really don't like each other!"

"It wasn't me. I didn't start it," Carrie protested, wondering why that made her sound like a six year old.

Ben stood up. "Okay, I hear you. You swear you didn't take the necklace?"

Carrie nodded. Her palms were sweating; her throat felt dry.

"So we have a mystery." The coach walked to the big window and gazed out over the patchwork of empty tennis courts. "It's kind of disappointing," he murmured.

Oh no, now came the part Carrie hated most—the how-could-you-let-me-down lecture. She knew the look that came with it and the sick feeling in the pit of her stomach.

"I hoped you'd do real well here at the Sherwood Academy," Ben went on. "It's your big chance to make tennis your life and have your mom and dad be real proud. Don't throw all that away."

"I won't. I'm not," Carrie said. "I didn't take the necklace!"

He shook his head, obviously unsure whether to believe her or not. "Okay, that's it for now. You get out of here, Carrie, and remember—stay out of trouble."

She stood up, still shaking. She was learning that when mud was thrown, it definitely stuck—big time!

"No more fights between you and Danielle," Ben warned. "Meanwhile, you understand that I have to ask Marie to search your room and Holly's room, to put you both in the clear."

So not fair! Carrie thought. But she bit her tongue and said nothing.

"Go!" Ben said finally. "Try not to let this have an impact on your game, okay?"

One final nod, and Carrie was out of Ben's office and running along the balcony. She hurried across the green lawn, ignoring the sprinkler and hardly noticing the cold water that soaked her hair and clothes. When she reached her room, she threw herself down on the bed and fell apart.

Why is this happening? she cried to herself. *What has Danielle got against me that makes her act like this?*

After a while she began to come around. *Come on,* she thought. *This is exactly what Danielle wants to happen—me sobbing in a corner, feeling sorry for myself. What I have to do is get out there and fight!*

But how? For a start, Ben had warned her to stay out of trouble. Next, she had a day's work on the court to get through before her match that evening.

Right! Carrie thought. *I can do this!* And with 15 minutes to get ready, she made a big effort to shower, dry her hair, and get down to the locker room to put on her tennis clothes. She must be out there on time, looking as if she had no worries, as if she was on top of her game.

"Hey, Carrie!" Bobby yelled as she ran toward the courts. He joined her, his short legs sprinting to keep up.

Maya and Michael Lewis also said hi, along with Leon, who gave her a high five. "Go, girl!" he grinned. He turned to Bobby and joked with him. "Hey, kid, you and me gotta play a tournament match later today. Are you ready to have your butt kicked?"

"Hey, back off!" Carrie told him. "He's

five whole years younger than you!"

"Yeah, I'm only little!" Bobby piped up.

Leon play fought his young opponent, tugging at his Disney T-shirt and then dodging out of reach. "Makes no difference," he insisted. "I'm gonna beat you anyway!"

"Shame on you!" Carrie laughed. *Will I ever be that focused?* she wondered as she ran onto the court.

On the far side of the court Danielle and Holly watched Carrie arrive. Carrie noticed that the two girls seemed to be talking about her as usual but decided to ignore them. Before long, Marie arrived, and the morning drill began.

Three long hours later, Carrie went for lunch. In spite of her interview with Ben in his office and the messy tears soon after, she now felt fine. She'd played well and enjoyed the thrill of hitting the ball in the center of the strings, making it zing off her racket. Now she felt like she could face anything Danielle might throw at her in their match later that day. She even said hi to Holly when she lined up behind her in the lunch line.

Holly frowned and turned away. Then suddenly she spun around to talk. "Did Marie search your room yet?" she hissed at Carrie, looking around to see who might be listening.

Carrie shrugged. "I don't know. But it sucks."

Holly nodded. "She's going to go through our private things."

Thanks to your precious friend, Danielle! Carrie thought. "Didn't you tell Ben that you didn't see the necklace?"

"Yes. I don't know if he believed me, though."

"The same with me." Carrie thought for a moment and then seized her chance. "Did the necklace really and truly get stolen?"

Holly looked shocked. "What are you saying?" she gasped.

But Carrie didn't have time to answer before Danielle swept through the door of the dining room and immediately cozied up to Holly.

"Hey!" she cried, grabbing her and dragging her away from Carrie. "I just heard from Ben that my mother called about my stolen necklace!" Danielle spoke loud enough for everyone in the room to hear. "She was furious. She told him that the necklace cost fifteen hundred dollars, and she wants him to bring in the police!"

The others gasped. Carrie froze. She'd thought things couldn't get worse, but now they just had.

"And will he?" Holly asked, her face pale with worry.

Danielle nodded. Giving Carrie an obvious stare, she let the whole world know who she thought the culprit was. "If the thief doesn't show herself before tomorrow morning, Ben will bring in the police!"

Chapter 10

"The key is to play Bobby as if I'm facing the world number one and this is a Grand Slam final!" Leon explained to Carrie. "Sure, he's only a little kid, but if I let that fact get inside my head and I start to go soft on him, then no way do I play my best tennis."

"So you intend to smash the poor kid off the court?"

Leon nodded. He led the way past the pool area. "Don't get me wrong—it's nothing personal against Bobby."

"Yeah, I like Bobby." Carrie spotted him already on court, knocking a ball around with Maya. Despite his spindly arms and legs, he could hit the ball hard and scoop up lots of incredible returns. "He's going to be a great player one day."

"Hey, kid!" Leon called as he joined Bobby on court. He gave him a high five and then prepared for battle.

Nothing personal, Carrie thought, agreeing with Leon's attitude. You could want to crush your opponent without letting emotions get in the way. *It's all about hitting the ball clean and hard, with maximum concentration.* Which was great, unless you were looking over your shoulder the whole day, waiting for a police car to arrive.

"Carrie, I need to search your room now," Marie had told her earlier that afternoon. The coach had sounded uneasy and asked Carrie to be present while she went through her things. "Sorry about this," she'd said. "I don't like it any more than you do, but I'm under orders from Ben, and he's under pressure from Danielle's mom."

Carrie had watched Marie empty her drawers and look in her closet without finding what she was supposed to be looking for.

"Okay, thanks," Marie had said abruptly, leaving with an embarrassed smile.

It had left a sour taste in Carrie's mouth and made her realize all over again that Danielle was set on wrecking her time here at the academy. For the rest of the afternoon Carrie had kept out of the French girl's way.

Now, though, as she watched Leon and Bobby begin their match, she noticed that Danielle and Holly had joined the small group of spectators and were cheering for Bobby, the underdog.

"Go, Bobby!" they chanted every time Leon went to serve.

Little Bobby pulled out some amazing returns.

"Bobby's so cute!" Danielle called. "Bobby, Bobby, Bobby, go, go, go!"

Soon everyone in the crowd had joined in against Leon, who was starting to miss his shots and lose his rhythm.

Danielle's even getting to Leon, Carrie realized. *When it comes to mind games, she is definitely the world number one!* And in less than 30 minutes she would have to face the French girl across the net.

"Sure, we're bringing in the police!" Danielle was telling Maya and a couple of others between games, as Leon and Bobby changed ends. "Marie hasn't found my necklace yet, but we figure it must still be hidden around the place somewhere."

"How come?" Maya asked, glancing quickly at Carrie.

"No one left the campus since it was stolen."

Carrie felt herself blush. She saw Danielle draw Maya and Holly into a huddle to discuss the so-called "crime."

Focus! she told herself. *Forget how much you would like to run away into a corner to curl up and die. Be tough. Never mind the personal stuff!*

"Leon leads by one set to love!" Marie called from the umpire's chair. Bobby had played his socks off, but Leon was proving to be too strong. The second set went quickly to three games to love.

I'll be on there in ten minutes! Carrie told herself, taking a deep breath. *I feel sick to my stomach and scared to death of Danielle, but I'm going to get out there and play the best I know how!*

On court little Bobby ran out of energy and lost two more games. Leon served for the match—three aces. Then at match point Bobby made a brilliant return and forced Leon to miss.

"Forty-fifteen!" Marie called.

Leon served again. The ball zoomed past a helpless Bobby.

"Game, set, and match!"

Leon jumped the net and high-fived with Bobby. He lifted him clear off his feet and swung him around. *Nothing personal!*

And then it was Carrie's turn, and she was on court, preparing to play Danielle, who looked perfect in her slinky, white dress, with gold hoop earrings glistening among her dark curls and bright pink wristbands setting off her Florida tan. Carrie tugged at her unruly fair hair to fix it more firmly into its ponytail.

"Go, Danielle!" Holly yelled as Marie called for the match to begin.

"Go, Carrie!" Leon retaliated.

Danielle had won the toss and served first. Carrie crouched to receive, telling herself to focus and stay calm. The serve flew past without Carrie even getting her racket to it—a winning ace!

"Yeah!" Holly clapped and cheered. The others joined in.

Danielle smashed and spun her way through the first game, which Carrie went through without winning a single point.

"Loser!" Danielle muttered under her breath as the two players changed ends.

Carrie's heart thudded. She prepared to serve.

"Wait!" Danielle called, stooping to tie her shoelace.

Carrie lost her rhythm and served awkwardly. Danielle flashed the ball back, but it bounced wide of the line. A point to Carrie at last! It felt good. On the next serve Danielle lost the point and then claimed a foot fault against Carrie, but Marie shook her head. That felt even better.

"Yeah, go Carrie!" Leon and Bobby shouted.

For the next 20 minutes Carrie and Danielle played hard, and the score rose to four-three in Danielle's favor.

"I said, *loser!*" Danielle repeated, as once again they changed ends. "The police are coming to get you!" she muttered. "How does it feel, *thief?*"

Carrie winced. She reached her service line, reeling from the insult. For a few moments she felt too dizzy to go on.

"Are you okay?" Marie called from the chair.

Nightmare! Everyone was staring. Across the net Danielle was smirking. Then something clicked in Carrie's head, and her dizziness cleared in an instant. She had that same feeling of certainty that she'd had during the standoff with her mum and dad.

What a witch! she thought, narrowing her eyes as if she was staring at her opponent down the barrel of a gun. *What a total, complete witch!*

Carrie threw the ball up in the air and served a missile. It shot past Danielle.

Forget the "nothing personal" routine—this is war! Carrie thought.

Pow! She served again. A second ace. Danielle looked rattled.

I did not steal your stupid necklace! Carrie thought every time she hit the ball. *So get a load of this!*

"Wow, look at Carrie!" Michael Lewis said in an awed voice.

"She's on fire!" Leon agreed.

Carrie prowled along the baseline, waiting for Danielle to serve. *No way are you going to beat me with your dirty tricks and your snide comments! I am going to play the best tennis of my life and thrash you off the court! Not for my parents or my coach or anyone else in this world—but for me!*

"I've never seen Carrie play like this before!" Maya declared.

"Hey, Carrie, you look like a winner!" Leon yelled.

Danielle frowned as she served. She was left standing by Carrie's bulletlike return.

"Thief!" she muttered at Carrie with every change of ends. "Wait until the police show up, loser!"

Carrie was leading by five games to four, powering her way to a one set to love lead.

Call me loser one more time, and I'll whack the ball straight at you! Carrie promised mentally. Anger fueled every winning shot she made.

"Carrie leads by three games to love,

second set, and by one set to love," Marie announced.

Danielle had just thrown her racket to the ground in disgust. She decided that it was time to play one last trick. On the next shot she reached for the ball, fell awkwardly, and didn't get up.

"Are you okay?" Marie asked, getting down from her chair and going to help the French girl.

Slowly, Danielle got to her feet. She put her weight onto her right foot, wincing as if she was in pain. "I twisted my ankle," she groaned.

"Do you want to pull out of the match?" the coach asked anxiously.

Danielle put on a show of being brave. "No, I'll finish," she said through gritted teeth.

That won't work on me! Carrie thought. She didn't trust a single thing Danielle did, playing the next two games like an out-and-out champion.

"Carrie leads by five games to love, second set!" Marie announced.

"Carrie! Carrie!" People were cheering and clapping. No one shouted for Danielle, not even Holly.

It was the French girl's turn to serve. Two double faults. Now Carrie just needed two points to win the match. She moved in on a weak serve, following Ben Sherwood's motto—go forward; never go back! A high return from Danielle allowed Carrie to smash the ball out of reach.

"Three match points!" Leon yelled.

"Carrie! Carrie!"

Danielle served, and Carrie returned safely. Danielle stepped in for a backhand, which she slammed into the net. Game, set, and match!

Victory! How sweet is this! Carrie ran forward to shake hands, but Danielle turned away. She limped toward the umpire's chair, complaining about her ankle.

"She's a sore loser!" Maya commented.

"Great game, Carrie!" Michael said.

Leon slapped Carrie on the back. "That sure looked personal to me!" he grinned.

"It was," Carrie admitted with an embarrassed grin.

It was then that she noticed Danielle had headed toward the wrong chair to pick up her tracksuit top, towel, and racket cases. Before Carrie could stop her, Danielle was busily zipping up Carrie's top and picking up her stuff.

"Hey!" Carrie pointed out the error.

Scowling, Danielle took off the top and threw it down on the ground.

"Drama queen," Leon muttered.

"She could at least say sorry," Maya frowned, slowly walking over to pick up Carrie's jacket. "Oh!" she said with a look of total surprise.

Everyone followed the direction of Maya's gaze to the crumpled white top on the ground and the glinting golden chain that had fallen out of Carrie's pocket.

Danielle stood back, staring at Carrie with pure hatred.

"Isn't this Danielle's necklace?" Maya gasped. She stooped to pick up the chain with its tiny, bright diamond pendant.

"Don't touch it!" Marie warned. She turned to Carrie.

Slowly, Carrie shook her head. "I don't . . . I have no idea . . . !"

All eyes were on the necklace.

"Holly, go and find Ben, please," Marie said in a tired voice. Like everyone else, she had drawn her own conclusion about how the necklace had come to be in Carrie's pocket.

"Carrie, you'd better wait in your room," she said.

Chapter 11

"You're finished!" Danielle told Carrie, her top lip curling up in scorn.

The campus was dark and deserted when the French girl dragged Holly with her to Carrie's room and knocked on the door. Carrie had ignored the knock, but now Danielle was on the balcony, peering in through the tall window.

"How does it feel to get thrown out of the best tennis academy in America?" she taunted.

"Leave me alone!" Carrie groaned, staring at Danielle and Holly through the gauzy screen. "Haven't you done enough?"

Danielle acted surprised. "Me? What did I do?"

"You know what you did!" Carrie retorted. She felt like a butterfly skewered on a collector's pin, struggling for life. "You planted that necklace in my pocket!"

"Ha ha!" Danielle came out with a fake laugh.

Holly frowned and looked uncomfortable. "Come on—let's go!" she urged.

Danielle shook her off. "Tell that to the police tomorrow morning!" she scoffed at Carrie. "Better make that *before* they throw you in a youth detention facility—see if anyone believes you!"

"Yeah!" Holly said faintly, still pulling on Danielle's arm. "How stupid can you be, Carrie Springsteen!"

"I'd say sleep well, but I figure the truth is, you won't be sleeping much tonight," Danielle said and laughed, enjoying every moment of Carrie's misery.

Through the screen Carrie saw the two girls step down onto the lawn. She ran after them, sliding the screen to one side and bursting onto the balcony.

"You set me up!" she yelled at Danielle. "It was because I outplayed you, and you lost the match in front of everyone. You couldn't stand that, could you, Danielle? Now this is your twisted way of getting back at me!"

"Ha!" the French girl gave a hollow laugh. "Say what you like; you're finished!"

"No! Whatever happens to me, I'm not the loser—you are!" Carrie shouted. Okay, her time here was over, and she was leaving in disgrace, but she wasn't about to go quietly. "You're a cheater and a liar!"

Danielle turned to argue, but this time Holly persuaded her to keep walking. Soon the lawn was empty and silent. Carrie stared out across the campus, toward the tennis courts and the beach beyond.

"Man, how low can you get?" a slow voice said.

Carrie blinked and then looked along the balcony. "Hi, Leon," she said with a sigh.

The tall Texan leaned against the white rail, his hands in his jeans pockets. "I knew Danielle was mean, but not that mean!"

"Did you hear that?" Carrie gasped.

Leon nodded. "Every word."

"And you believe me?"

A second nod.

Turning to stare up at the stars and moon, Carrie thanked him. Her dreams might lie shattered in thousands of pieces, but at least she had made one good friend who still believed in her. She glanced back at him. "You've been my friend from the start. It means a lot to me," she murmured.

Danielle was right about one thing—that night Carrie hardly slept a wink. Instead she tossed on her bed, rehearsing the story that she would tell the police in Ben's office first thing tomorrow.

"I didn't steal the necklace . . . Marie searched my room, and it wasn't there . . . Danielle slipped it into my tracksuit pocket when no one was looking!"

"Why would Danielle do that?" the cop would ask.

"Because I beat her at tennis!" Carrie would say.

Time and time again she ran this scene in her head, and every time it stopped here, with the cop shaking his head and looking at Ben Sherwood. "Help me out with this," he would say to the coach. "Is this kid crazy, or what?"

In the end Carrie couldn't bear it anymore, and at the first signs of a pink dawn in the sky she got up and went to the beach.

She walked along the shore, gazing out across the calm sea, trying to control the storm of emotions going on inside her.

"I could have been good," she said out loud, sighing over the future that was never going to be. "I know I could have made it to the top."

She imagined the crowds at Wimbledon,

the cameras flashing, the attention of the world on her wherever she went. And she remembered her old horoscope—"You're a winner, Leo, and you have big dreams."

Had! she thought bitterly. *Had big dreams!*

Right now, half a world away from home, after a big fight with her mum and dad, she had lost everything, and she was scared.

Turning back to face the worst day of her life, Carrie was surprised to see two other shadowy figures on the otherwise empty beach.

One was Ben Sherwood, dressed in exercise clothes, obviously setting out on his early-morning jog. The other looked like Holly Jordan.

Carrie's heart missed a beat, wondering how to avoid them.

She looked again. Holly seemed to be making gestures and talking loudly. Ben was shaking his head, standing with his hands on his hips. Suddenly, Holly spotted Carrie and started to run toward her.

"Don't go away. Carrie, come here!" Holly begged. "You have to help me explain!"

"What's to explain?" Carrie retorted, still intent on heading off in the other direction. "I've said all I have to say. No one believed me."

Holly chased her. "No, listen. Come and talk to Ben."

The coach watched from a distance and then started to slowly walk toward the girls.

"What's going on?" Carrie asked.

"I've told him the truth!" Holly confessed.

Stunned, Carrie took a step back. "Say that again!" she stammered.

"I just told Ben what Danielle did to you. Honestly, Carrie, I haven't slept a wink, knowing how she stitched you up!"

"You knew?" Carrie echoed.

Holly nodded. "Right from the start. At first I thought it was a laugh, but then it got serious. I told Danielle to stop, but she wouldn't!"

Carrie stared. "You thought it was funny?"

"I'm sorry!" Holly cried. "I feel so bad about it."

"Why did you go along with it in the first place?" Trying to gather her thoughts, Carrie saw that Ben was nearby, overhearing every word.

"I guess I thought that it was a way to get you out of my hair." Holly's face was pale, her voice halting. "Back home, you always beat me when we play in tournaments. I'm only the County Champion because you weren't there!"

Carrie nodded. Yeah, she could understand how Holly had been dragged into this mess.

"Okay, I've heard enough." Ben stepped forward and took control. "Holly, you did the right thing in the end, and for that I'm grateful."

Carrie nodded. "Thanks," she murmured. She saw from Ben's face that there would be no police, no more disgrace. The shattered pieces of her dream flew back together.

"I'm just so sorry!" Holly told her. "After the County Championship I felt such a buzz from being the winner, and I didn't want to let go of that. I told myself I would do practically anything to stay on top, instead of losing to you the way I normally do."

"It's okay. I understand," Carrie said quietly.

Holly shook her head. "It's not okay. Once I got to the academy and learned that you were here on a scholarship, I was totally jealous, and I let the whole thing get out of hand . . ."

"Hey, guys." Ben stepped in as Holly broke down in tears. "The important thing to realize is that, from here on in, you two can be rivals, but you can also be friends."

Carrie nodded. "That's fine by me," she assured Holly.

"Really?" Holly braced herself to look Carrie in the eye. "We can honestly be friends?"

Carrie grinned at her. She was looking ahead at the future, confidently seeing a picture of tennis stardom lighting up her world. "Sure," she said to Holly. "But I'll tell you one thing—it won't stop me from kicking . . ."

". . . my butt!" Holly grinned back.

It was the end of the road for Danielle. Later that day her angry mother arrived in a silver Mercedes to take her away.

"Back to Paris!" Leon commented happily. He lounged in the clubhouse doorway with a bunch of other kids, watching the French girl's sudden exit from the world of major-league tennis. "So now she can do all the shopping she wants!"

Carrie and Holly didn't join in the laughter. They watched Danielle lug her bags to the car, saw the cold way that her mother glared at her, and knew that Danielle had a tough time ahead.

Ben Sherwood and Marie were on hand to watch them leave. They talked seriously with Danielle's mother, while Danielle loaded the trunk of the car.

"I feel kind of sorry for her," Maya said.

"No way!" Michael argued. "She had it coming!"

Ben and Marie stepped back while Danielle's mother got into the car. Danielle slung her rackets onto the backseat and then slid in beside her mother. She kept her head down and didn't look back once as the car swished away down the drive.

Chapter 12

Work, work, and work! For the rest of the month Carrie trained "The Sherwood Way." She improved her forehand and learned to put topspin on her second serve. With Marie, she watched her videotapes and analyzed her tactics.

With each day that passed, Carrie improved her game.

"Work, work, and still more work!" Ben Sherwood reminded her at the end of an especially hard day. Carrie was sitting under a palm tree by the pool when the coach came to join her. "That's what it takes to reach the top."

Feeling guilty for slacking, Carrie sprang onto her feet. "I was planning to play

Michael in a practice match before the evening meal," she explained.

"Hey, kid. Chill." For once Ben sat beside her on one of the striped loungers. He put his hands behind his head and lay back to soak up the evening sun.

"Chill?" Carrie repeated.

"Yeah, you know—R-E-L-A-X." He spelled it out for her.

Carrie stared at him. Had the toughest coach in tennis just used the "R" word?

He grinned back at her. "Now that you've taken the academy's work ethic on board, it's time I let you in on a secret."

"It is?" Carrie couldn't help sitting there openmouthed.

"Listen to me. Sure, you have to work hard and give the game of tennis everything you've got. But at the same time you need to know how to switch off and just hang out."

"I do?"

Ben nodded. "It's a question of balance.

Work hard, play hard. Look at Leon, for instance."

Across the pool the tall Texan was fooling around with Bobby, playing foosball, spinning the tiny plastic players and yelling when he scored a goal. Michael and Maya came across the lawn and joined in the fun.

"Leon has great talent and works hard, but he also knows how to party," Ben said.

"Yeah, he's cool," Carrie agreed.

"So he's a kid who won't burn out by the time he's twenty years old," the coach explained. He raised his sunglasses onto his forehead and stared hard at her. "Get it?"

Slowly, she nodded. *Wow, how cool is this! I can play tennis and still chill with my friends! I can party with Liv and Mandi and Alice after all, and tennis doesn't have to be the menace that ruins my social life! How come my mum and dad never told me that?* she wondered.

Ben stood up and fixed his sunglasses back over his eyes. "I'll leave you to think about that," he told her as he strolled on.

Carrie thought. Yes, it was definitely time to say good-bye to social life sadness and hello to fun with friends. And there was no time like the present. She had a few spare minutes to make a phone call before she changed into her tennis outfit.

"Hey, Liv!"

"Hey!" Liv sounded thrilled to hear from her. "How's the academy? How long before you're out of there?"

"Two days. I fly overnight Friday. I'm back on Saturday."

"Cool. Has it been a total slog?"

"Pretty much. But I'm having a good time too. Like, it's ninety-eight degrees, and I've just been sunbathing, lying by the pool, looking out at the blue, blue ocean. Life doesn't get much tougher than that!"

"Jeez, I'm jealous!" Liv groaned. Then she remembered something. "Hey, there's a party this Saturday night at Hannah Laker's house. Oh . . . I guess you won't be able to make it, though."

Work hard, play hard—that's what Ben had said. "Sure I will!" Carrie told Liv without a moment's hesitation. "What time does it start?"

"Seven-thirty."

"Cool, Liv," Carrie said. "Tell Mandi and Alice I'll see you all there!"

Before she took the plane home, however, there was one more tennis match for Carrie to play.

"I reached the final," she told her mum on the phone. "I just knocked out my best friend, Leon, in the semi."

"That's great, honey! What was the score?" Since the argument over the phone, Eva had been cautious, trying her best not to upset Carrie.

"Six-four, seven-five. It was a tough match." Leon had thrown everything at her—

lobbing and playing mega passing shots, using topspin, and rushing the net. But Carrie had stood up to the attacks and outplayed him in the end.

"Great match," he'd told her as they shook hands at the net. "You played real good!"

But he hadn't left her floating on a high for long. "You comin' back next summer?" he'd asked.

Carrie had picked up her towel and rubbed the sweat from her forehead. "Don't know. Maybe." *I hope so—I really do!* she'd said to herself. "Why do you ask?"

Leon had stuck his face right into hers. His eyes sparkled with fun even though he'd just lost. "'Cause if you do, and I'm still on the circuit . . ."

"Yeah?" she'd prompted, laughing back at him.

He struck a pose, giving himself big shoulders and ape-man arms. "Prepare to die!" he'd roared.

★ ★ ★

"That was a close match," Carrie's mum said now. "So, who do you play in the final?"

"You'll never believe it." Carrie laughed at the way the draw had worked out. "Go on, take a guess."

"Not Holly Jordan?"

"Good guess!"

"Here, let me speak to my girl." As usual, Martin Springsteen butted in. "You know you can beat Holly," he insisted. "I don't want to hear any more talk of getting injured or of you quitting tennis. You go out there and play to win!"

Carrie bit her lip and narrowed her eyes, about to give her dad a fight. *Don't boss me around. Don't push me, or I'll quit!* But instead she held back. *What's the point?* she thought. *Dad is the way he is, and he's never going to change!* "I'll do my best," she promised him instead.

★ ★ ★

"The point is, *I've* changed," she said out loud, staring at her own reflection in the locker-room mirror.

She saw a tall, slim, tanned figure in a neat tennis dress and pure-white shoes, her fair hair pulled back into a high ponytail. "I look like a player who wants to win after all," she told herself, psyching herself up before she went out to play her archrival. "I *am* the one to watch! I am a winner!"

Carrie walked onto court to play the final with her head held up high. Across the net Holly bounced a ball on the baseline, nervously waiting for play to begin.

"Carrie Springsteen to serve!" Marie announced from the umpire's chair.

"Go, Carrie! Go, Holly!" Everyone was there to cheer on their favorite on this scorching last day of summer school.

"Play!" Marie called.

Carrie threw the ball into the dazzling sun. She squinted as she swung her racket and hit the ball awkwardly. *Plop!*—her first serve landed in the net. The second was slower but more accurate.

Whiz! Holly pounced on the short ball and whipped it back over the net. Carrie scrambled to return it, giving her opponent a second chance. This time Holly volleyed the ball way out of Carrie's reach.

"Love-fifteen!" Marie called.

It was a bad start, and soon it got worse. With the sun in her eyes, Carrie failed to get any first serves in, letting Holly romp into the lead. Then they changed ends, and Holly dealt better with the glare of the sun. Soon she was leading by three games to love.

Nightmare! Carrie said to herself, sitting on a chair by the umpire's seat at the next change of ends. *I'm playing terribly!* She thought of all the training she'd done with Marie and Ben, all the practice she'd put in here at the academy.

Yet suddenly it felt as if she'd never held a tennis racket before.

The crowd clapped and cheered as the two players got onto their feet to play on. "Hey, Carrie!" Leon yelled above the rest.

Carrie glanced over her shoulder. There was Leon standing next to Ben Sherwood, doing his stupid ape-arms thing.

"It's a jungle out there!" he reminded her. "It's dog-eat-dog, man!"

She nodded, realizing that she had to fight back during this next game or else would probably say good-bye to the set. But she was at the bad end again, with the sun in her eyes.

"You gotta kick butt, girl!" Leon yelled. He saw her pause before she threw the ball to serve. "Go, Carrie, go!"

She bounced the ball—once, twice, three times. Ready! She threw it into the air, and with surefire accuracy, she slammed it into play.

Holly dived for Carrie's serve and missed.

"Fifteen-love!" Marie called.

An ace—that felt good! Carrie served a second ace and set the crowd cheering. Leon yelled the loudest. Ben stood and nodded.

Three games to one, three-two, three-all. The players were equal, and it was halfway through the first set. Now Holly was in trouble with the sun and missing her serves. She went down three-four and then three-five. Carrie served for the set and won.

Then they were into the second set, and every muscle was straining to reach the ball. Carrie ran, twisted, and turned. She scooped up low shots and jumped up high to retrieve Holly's lobs. "Good shot!" she called when her opponent sneaked a low ball past her. The crowd groaned when Holly slipped and fell and then cheered when she got onto her feet with no harm done.

The score seesawed, first in Holly's favor and then in Carrie's. Soon it was five games to four to Carrie.

"Go, Carrie!" Leon and Bobby yelled as the players changed ends.

I can do this! she told herself, sweating in the heat. She wiped the handle of her racket on her towel and walked out onto the court. *I came all this way to Florida to make my dream come true. No way am I going to let it slip away!*

She served. Holly returned down the forehand line. Carrie stretched and whacked it diagonally across the court. This time Holly couldn't get her racket anywhere near it.

First point in the vital game went to Carrie. But Holly pulled back with three straight points.

"Fifteen-forty!" Marie announced.

Leon and Bobby groaned.

"I can do it!" Carrie muttered. She served one ace and then another.

"Deuce!"

Two more points, and I win the match!

Carrie focused on her serve. It crashed down into Holly's court, but Holly got her racket to it and returned it low and fast. Carrie sprinted to retrieve it, pulling a crosscourt shot out of nowhere. The return left Holly rooted to the spot.

"Advantage, Carrie!" Marie called.

Match point! Carrie stood poised on the baseline. The ball went high up into the air. She leaned back and brought her racket down in an unbelievable serve that skimmed the net and left Holly standing— another ace!

There was a huge cheer. Carrie ran and jumped the net. She hugged Holly, and the two girls left the court arm in arm.

"Game, set, and match to Carrie Springsteen!" Marie announced.

"You came through," Ben told Carrie as her stay at the academy came to its end. "And I don't just mean winning the final. I mean, it was tough back there for a while with Danielle and her dirty tricks, but you didn't cave in. You showed guts!"

Carrie grinned. She was carrying her rackets onto the minibus that was taking her, Holly, Leon, Bobby, and a couple of others to the airport. In less than 12 hours she would be home.

"You proved me wrong," the great Ben Sherwood told her with a smile.

Wow, that must be a first! "How come?" she asked, beaming back at him.

"You want me to give it to you straight?" he asked.

Carrie nodded.

"When you first came, I doubted whether you had the necessary mental toughness to make it to the top."

"And now?" Before she stepped onto the bus and back into a world where the sun didn't always shine, she wanted to hear it from Ben's own lips. She knew that they would be words she would treasure for the rest of her life.

"Now, you have the will to win," Ben told her. "I see it in your eyes and your body language—you have the makings of a champion!"

Carrie took a deep breath, shook the coach's hand, and got onto the bus. She turned on the top step and looked down at him. "See you next year," she said.

Want to read more exciting sports stories?
Here's the first chapter from Donna King's
Double Twist*!*

"Most kids spend their summer holiday sunbathing on a beach in Spain," Jack Lee muttered to his younger sister Laura. "So how come you're standing here shivering at the side of an ice rink?"

"Because I'm a child star!" Laura said with a grin. "A genius on ice!"

Jack zipped his jacket up to his chin. "Says who?"

"Says Mum." Laura waited impatiently for the public session to end so that she could skate onto the ice for her private coaching lesson with Vera Mozer while Jack went to play soccer. Their mum was due to pick her up later. "Where's Patrick?" Jack wondered out loud.

"Don't worry—he'll be here." Laura watched the little kids on the ice. They whizzed around the rink like demons, in and out of the grown-ups, who wobbled and crashed down like dominoes. One or two older kids tried out turns and spins, taking the whole thing more seriously. "Patrick's never late," she added.

Jack glanced back at the entrance, spied Laura's tall, serious ice-dancing partner, and yelled out his name. "Hey, Patrick, over here!" Now he could dash.

Patrick joined them. He was wearing a thick padded jacket and a scarf wound high around his neck. "Hey," he said quietly.

"Where are your folks?" Jack asked.

"Mum and Dad? They dropped me off and then went to the bank. They'll be back in a few minutes."

"So is it okay if I head off?"

Laura and Patrick nodded. Laura was grinning at the sight of another grown-up biting the dust. A middle-aged woman squealed as she went down, smack on her bottom. "Oops!"

"Don't laugh!" Patrick bit his lip and looked away.

"She's down! Now she's up and brushing the ice off herself. . . . Oops, she's down again!" Eventually, the poor woman made it to the edge of the rink and clung onto the rail. "Why isn't she at home watching TV and knitting woolly scarves for her grandkids?"

"Laura!" Patrick shook his head, glad when the siren sounded for everyone to clear the ice. At least now Laura wouldn't be able to make fun of the old ladies.

"Lighten up!" Laura giggled, saying hi to a couple of kids she knew from school as they came off the ice. "Hey, Georgina! Hey, Abi!"

"Are you here to practice?" Abi asked as she bent down to take off her skates.

"Yep. Why?"

"Just wondered if you wanted to join us at the café."

"Thanks. I'd love to, but we've got a big

competition coming up. Gotta keep on practicing those twizzles!"

"Poor you!" Abi grinned. "Where are you jetting off to this time?"

"Montreal, in just under a month."

"Canada?" Abi's jaw dropped. "Wow!"

"Junior Grand Prix," Patrick chipped in. "We're in the running for a medal if we work hard."

Georgina tugged on her friend's arm. "C'mon—I'm starving!"

"Well, good luck!" Abi said to Laura and Patrick. "Wow, Canada . . . cool!"

"Laura, you need more leg and foot extension in that third section!" Vera's eagle eyes didn't miss a thing. "Patrick, you were too close to the boards on the synchronized leg swing!"

"Sorry!" Laura told her partner under her breath. They'd been working nonstop for an hour, and her concentration was beginning to dip. "This compulsory section isn't my thing."

"We've still got to get it right," he insisted. "Let's do it one more time."

They took up their positions in the center of the empty rink. Their coach watched from the barrier. "I'm asking a lot of you with this paso doble," she called. "You have to dance exactly to the beat and keep the Latin spirit going, while getting those twizzles right and leading smoothly into the lift at the same time. Okay, try again!"

Laura heard the music start. She noticed Patrick's mum and dad behind Vera and then her own mum joining them. With this audience, she knew she'd better get her act together. *Leg and foot extension!* she reminded herself. *Synchronized leg swings!*

Together, she and Patrick sprang into action. This rhythm was tricky—it was fast and dramatic, and if you missed a beat, the whole thing went wrong.

"Laura, your foot was loose on that

diagonal sequence. Patrick, you overrotated on the landing of that double throw loop!" Once more Vera picked up every tiny error and bellowed out across the ice. It was what you'd expect from a woman who had been an Olympic ice-dancing gold-medal winner herself. She never let you get away with one single thing.

Laura linked hands with Patrick for another lift, using their speed to get her off the ground and spreading her arms wide as he hoisted her into the air. She saw the overhead lights start to blur as Patrick spun her; she remembered her leg and foot extension and felt herself lowered and her blades make contact with the ice.

"Good!" Vera called.

Laura made eye contact with her partner and grinned. *Definite praise from the great ex-champion—wow!*

They got their leg lines sorted out on the next turn sequence and then made their grand finish, arms flung wide, backs arched like Spanish bullfighters.

"Whoa!" Laura gasped. She relaxed her position and gave her mum a quick wave. "Patrick, I think we just did the whole thing without one mistake!"

He nodded happily, his gray eyes gleaming, waving at his own mum and dad as he and Laura skated toward Vera to hear her verdict.

Their coach gave them a hard look from underneath her fur hat, standing with her hands in her pockets and clicking her tongue against the roof of her mouth. "Not bad," she said slowly in her thick accent. "But not the best. Now, go and do it all over again!"